HODDER CHILDREN'S BOOKS

First published in Great Britain in 2015 by Hodder and Stoughton

5 7 9 10 8 6 4

A CIP catalogue record for this book
is available from the British Library.

ISBN 978 1 444 91623 2

Printed in China

Hodder Children's Books Australia
Level 17/207 Kent Street
Sydney, NSW 2000

Hodder Children's Books
An imprint of
Hachette Children's Group
Part of Hodder and Stoughton
Carmelite House
50 Victoria Embankment
London EC4Y 0DZ

An Hachette UK Company
www.hachette.co.uk

www.hachettechildrens.co.uk

What any author wants is for his books to become dog-eared and familiar. I've been lucky enough that my very young readers are particularly adept at giving their books doggy ears in no time at all.

And of all my books, perhaps it's those about Kipper that get the doggiest ears of all, which I guess is kind of appropriate.

*Mick Inkpen*

# Kipper's
# Christmas Eve

## Mick Inkpen

Hodder
Children's
Books

'Which is best?' said Kipper to himself. 'Christmas Day? Or Christmas Eve?' He reached the top of Big Hill and stopped. 'Presents? Or expecting presents?'

And then, because he was too excited to decide, he just whooped, and went charging down the slope towards the wood.

It was Christmas Eve and he was looking for a Christmas tree to take home.

In the middle of the
wood was a little fir tree.
'That's the one!' said Kipper.
He dug away the snow with
his spade. Then he grabbed the
tree and pulled. It wouldn't come.
He pushed it, shook it, twisted
and lifted it. Then he looped his
scarf around it,
and heaved,
and heaved,
and heaved
until...

**I**t did!

'I wonder what Father Christmas will bring me?' thought Kipper as he dragged the tree home.

This year, as every year, Kipper couldn't think what sort of present he would like.

'I expect I'll know what I want when I see what it is,' said Kipper.

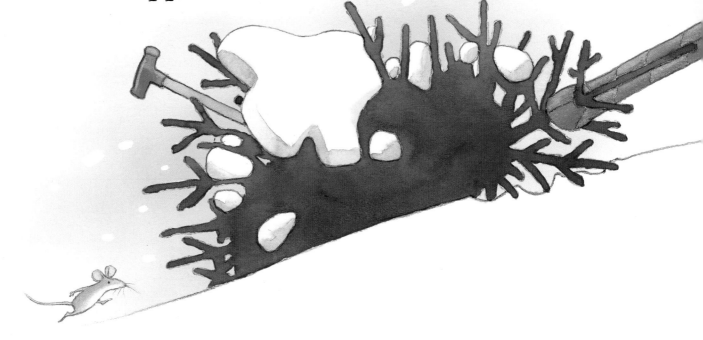

He was still thinking about presents when he saw Pig and his little cousin Arnold coming over the hill.

'Hello Kipper!' said Pig. 'Do you want a hand with that?'

Pig tied his own scarf to the fir tree and together they heaved it up the slope, while Arnold toddled along behind, sucking his thumb.

He was pointing at something in the tree. But Kipper and Pig were too busy talking about presents to notice.

At Kipper's house they stood the tree in a bucket. Arnold peered into the branches, walking round and round the tree, until he bumped into a pile of Christmas presents.

One of them had a label with his name on it. 'Happy Christmas, Arnold. Love from Kipper,' it said.

'You mustn't open that until tomorrow!' said Pig.

But he already had.

Kipper's present to Arnold was
a reindeer hat.

'The red nose lights up!' said Kipper
enthusiastically. 'And it flashes too!'
But then his face fell. He had forgotten to
buy the batteries.

Arnold didn't mind.
He loved his hat,
even without its
battery operated
flashing
red nose.

'That reminds me!' said Pig.
'I haven't wrapped up your
present yet!' So Pig went home, while
Arnold stayed with Kipper to help him
decorate the Christmas tree.

'What shall we put on top, Arnold?'
said Kipper. 'A snowman? Or a star?'

But Arnold didn't seem to be
interested in the decorations.

Arnold climbed on to the stool, took off his hat, and plopped it over the mouse. The stool wobbled and fell over.

'Are you all right, Arnold?'
said Kipper. Arnold sat up
and pointed.

Kipper looked at the reindeer hat
sitting on top of the Christmas tree.

'Clever old you!' he said to Arnold.
'It's just right!'

And so it was.

Just as they finished decorating the tree the doorbell rang. It was Tiger. He had come to wish Kipper a Merry Christmas. And to throw a snowball at him.

Pig arrived too.
'Sorry it's a bit lumpy,' said Pig,
handing Kipper his present. 'I'm not very
good at wrapping things up.'

'I like lumpy presents,' said Kipper.
'It makes you wonder what's inside.'

'Time to go home,' said Pig to Arnold. Kipper took Arnold's hat from the tree and gave it back to him. Arnold looked inside. There was no mouse.

'Merry Christmas, Kipper!' said Pig.

'Merry Christmas, Kipper!' said Tiger.

'Merry Christmas, everyone!' said Kipper, as they walked out into the snow. 'Look out for Father Christmas!'

Arnold waved and looked inside his hat once more, just to make sure there really was nothing there.

'I think Christmas Eve is best,' said Kipper, putting out some biscuits for Father Christmas. He pegged Sock Thing to his basket with a note.

'To Father Christmas.
Anything please. Thank you.
Love from Kipper.'

He pulled the blanket up and lay staring out of the window at the stars.

He was wide awake.
He wasn't sleepy at all.
He couldn't wait for
Father Christmas
to come...

Nor could the mouse...

. . . and nor could Arnold.

'My children absolutely LOVE all of Mick Inkpen's books, and I still love reading Kipper to them, even when it's for the hundredth time. . .'

CRESSIDA COWELL

'He is the perfect pup to grow up with. . .'

HILARY MCKAY

'Storytelling at its best.' DAVID MELLING